LOOKING AT PAINTINGS

Musicians

Banjo Player, 1862
D. Morrill, American (active 1850–70)

LOOKING AT PAINTINGS

Musicians

Peggy Roalf

Series Editor
Jacques Lowe

Design
Joseph Guglietti

Hyperion Books for Children
New York

A
JACQUES LOWE
VISUAL ARTS PROJECTS
BOOK

Text © 1993 by Jacques Lowe Visual Arts Projects Inc.
A Jacques Lowe Visual Arts Projects Book

Printed in Italy

FIRST EDITION

1 3 5 7 9 10 8 6 4 2

Roalf, Peggy.
Musicians/Peggy Roalf — 1st ed.
p. cm. — (Looking at paintings)
Includes index.
Summary: Presents 2000 years of art history
through a series of paintings of musicians.
ISBN 1-56282-532-1 (trade) — ISBN 1-56282-533-X (lib. bdg.)
1. Music in art — Juvenile literature. 2. Musicians in art — Juvenile
literature. [1. Musicians in art. 2. Music in art — Juvenile literature.
3. Painting — History. 4. Art appreciation.]
I. Title. II. Series: Roalf, Peggy. Looking at paintings.
ML85. R62 1993
758'.978 — dc20   93-15555
CIP
MN AC

Original design concept by Amy Hill

Contents

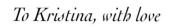

To Kristina, with love

Introduction

LOOKING AT PAINTINGS is a series of books about the artistic process of seeing, thinking, and painting. Painters have created scenes depicting musicians for more than two thousand years to express joy, beauty, and sometimes, despair. In ancient times, an anonymous Roman artist created an elegant mural depicting a woman playing the cithara to decorate a luxurious country villa. In *The Musicians*, Caravaggio took a fresh view of a traditional theme in painting. His lifelike portrayal, with gleaming light and smoldering shadows, introduced a new style of painting and a new era in art, called the baroque period. In seventeenth-century Holland, Judith Leyster's artistry transformed a portrait of a young flute player from an ordinary scene into a masterpiece through the lively arrangement of lines that radiate through the picture in a circular path.

In *Green Violinist*, Marc Chagall's dreamlike fiddler on the roof expresses the joy music brought to Jewish people who were persecuted by the Russian czars. African-American painter William H. Johnson used bold outlines, graphic shapes resembling cutouts, and a few strong colors to capture Harlem's sidewalk culture in *Street Musicians*.

In *Le-lo-lai*, Lorenzo Homar expressed his despair over the poverty afflicting children in a Puerto Rico slum through the contrast between their crowns, painted with real gold and silver, and their skinny hands playing a guitar and a guiro. Hung Liu, who emigrated from China to the United States, created a modern shrine for people to offer their thoughts about history and culture in a painting inspired by an antique photograph of four musicians.

Great artists have revealed their character and their innermost feelings in portrayals of musicians. When you look with imagination and insight at the people who create music in your life, you can see with the eyes of a painter.

CITHARA PLAYER, detail, about 50–40 B.C.
Unknown Roman artist, fresco, 73½" high

In the first century B.C., a wealthy Roman named Fannius Synistor owned a luxurious villa in Boscoreale, located a few miles from Mount Vesuvius. He hired painters to decorate the walls with murals depicting historical and mythological figures. A Macedonian queen playing the cithara, an instrument that sounds like a harp, was one of eight scenes adorning a large banquet hall.

The red background and thronelike chair create a mood of warmth and luxury.

On 24 August, A.D. 79, the sky over Boscoreale turned black with cinders from the volcanic eruption of Mount Vesuvius. The entire region was buried under a deep layer of molten lava, which hardened into an impenetrable mass. All life ceased. Boscoreale and Villa Fannius were entombed for almost two thousand years until *archaeologists* unearthed the house and this majestic *mural* in 1900.

The artist who created this mural demonstrates the influence of classical Greek sculpture on Roman painting. The instrumentalist's face has the volume, or sense of mass, of a *portrait* carved from marble. The painter first painted the shaded areas of the face with a russet tone and then applied a thin layer of flesh-colored paint that permits the *shading* to show through. With a series of parallel white strokes on top of the deep tones, the painter gave a solid look to the woman's cheeks, nose, and neck. The artist created an air of tranquillity through his skill in combining a narrow range of pigments mined from the earth: ocher, umber, sienna, minium red, and zinc white.

This mural was done in *fresco*, a method of painting directly onto wet *plaster*. Because the paint and plaster bonded together as they dried, the painting survived. Although the plaster on which it was painted is now cracked, the feeling of luxury and elegance lives on.

THE CHRISTMAS PICTURE, detail from the Isenheim Altarpiece, about 1510–15
Matthias Grünewald, German (1455–1528), on panel, 132" high

Matthias Grünewald was a master artist and architect in sixteenth-century Germany. His greatest creation is an altarpiece for the Antonian monastery in Isenheim, Alsace, which retells the birth and death of Jesus Christ in paintings.

Before the advent of books and general education, religious paintings, such as this altarpiece, were used to teach people who could not read. Hinged, movable panels revealed three different scenes that depicted stories from the New Testament. The paintings reminded people that even though life was difficult, those who had faith would be rewarded with life after death. On days of celebration, a tragic scene of the Crucifixion, or death of Christ, was pulled away to uncover a glorious image of the Nativity, or birth of Christ.

In Grünewald's animated portrayal, an orchestra of angels proclaims the wondrous birth. Cecilia, patron saint of musicians and singers, leads the orchestra from the viola da gamba, a cellolike instrument. Every *line* shaping Cecilia's figure and features vibrates with energy and life. Grünewald used delicate tones of rose and yellow to create the effect of light radiating from within. He formed the sweeping folds of Cecilia's robe with gleaming cerulean *shadows*. The vermilion robe worn by the archangel Gabriel, at right, draws attention to a pageant of cherubs and seraphim hovering in the distant sky.

In *contrast* to the radiant portrayal of Cecilia, Grünewald's haunting image of the dark fallen angel, Lucifer, at top left, adds mystery and drama to this extraordinary painting of the first Christmas.

Until the twentieth century, this masterpiece of religious painting was attributed to Grünewald's more famous contemporary, Albrecht Dürer.

Using a technique called trompe l'oeil, Grünewald tricks the eye into believing that the scene is framed by an elaborately carved wooden arch.

HEAVENLY JOYS COME TO EARTH, 1588
Painting from *Anvari's Divan* attributed to Khem Karan, ink, watercolor, gold, and silver on paper, 5½" x 2⅞"

Akbar the Great was the third Mogul emperor of northern India. During his reign in the sixteenth century, he founded a painting studio in which more than one hundred artists created illustrated albums of poetry and of history called illuminated manuscripts. *Anvari's Divan* is a palm-size volume of poetry created for Akbar to enjoy when he traveled. On this page, Akbar himself is cast as the twelfth-century poet Anvari. Among the instruments portrayed are flutes called *bansuri*, a tambourine called a *duff*, and large castanets called *kartals*. Together, they bring the "heavenly joys" of music to Akbar's court.

Several artists working together under Akbar's supervision brought this performance to life on the tiny page. A master artist named Khem Karan envisioned the entire scene. He first made a *drawing* in which the figures and the *composition* were carefully designed on heavy paper. Khem's drawing, called a *cartoon*, was then transferred onto the actual book pages and painted in watercolor by an unnamed artist. A third artist inscribed the text in calligraphy, or beautiful writing, as seen in the small illustration.

Khem chose a high vantage point that enabled him to fill the picture with activity. Cool greens in the flat, open floor area and in the distant landscape contrast with warm reds and yellows in the figures, creating an airy, spacious feeling. Using delicate kitten-hair brushes and paint made of gold and silver, the colorist embellished the musicians, the emperor, and the furnishings with intricate miniature *designs*.

Akbar's great painting studio was kept alive by his son, Prince Salim, who worked at his father's side during the planning of *Anvari's Divan*.

Delicate gold borders and text inscribed on blocks of gold leaf make the painting stand out against the paper, which is painted to resemble marble.

خواب خرگوش غیر کین ترا
سیر نشسته چو رو به ماد

بنده باچه خر بطست امروز
جون خواند کلاب افتاده

THE MUSICIANS, about 1595
Caravaggio, born Michelangelo Merisi, Italian (1573–1610), oil on canvas,
34⅝" x 45⅝"

Talent, skill, and dedication were not enough to ensure success for an ambitious painter in sixteenth-century Italy. Caravaggio lived in poverty until he found a *patron*, Cardinal Francesco Maria del Monte, head of the painting academy in Rome. Until then, Caravaggio survived by copying devotional paintings for St. Peter's Basilica and by working as a master artist's assistant. *The Musicians* is the first work Caravaggio created for the cardinal.

Caravaggio created a feeling of depth through the dark russet tones with which he painted his self-portrait.

Caravaggio based this picture on the allegory of music as the inspiration for harmony and love. He expressed the joy of song through the earthy portrayal of four men clothed in ancient Greek costume. By depicting men rather than women and by including a lute, the most popular stringed instrument of the time, Caravaggio gave this traditional Renaissance theme a contemporary look.

Caravaggio created a dramatic mood by choosing a vantage point that places the viewer among the musicians, as though we have encountered the group by chance, and through the pronounced *contrast* of light and *shadow*, called chiaroscuro. He formed velvety shadows defining the lutenist's face by painting the deep tones first. The deep shadows shaping the musician's cheeks, nose, and chin create a powerful sculptural effect. Rosy *shading* and gleaming *highlights* give the lute player's eyes intensity and depth. Russet shadows engulf the musician in the *background*, which is the artist's *self-portrait*, forming a contrast with the lutenist's pale complexion.

Caravaggio's emotional pictures, drawn from life and intensified by his vision, broke with the idealizing tradition of Renaissance painting and ushered in the baroque period in art.

THE STORY OF HONDA HEIHACHIRO, detail, early 17th century
Unknown Japanese artist, ink, colors, and gold leaf on paper, 28⅝" high

Japanese art and culture were redefined following the chance arrival of a shipwrecked Portuguese sailor who introduced gunpowder and firearms to Japan in 1508. Sixty years later, powerful warlords, called shoguns, newly armed with cannons and rifles, began a bloody civil war for control of the provinces.

This scene of samisen players and their audience seated before a large landscape painting shows how screens were used to make an enormous room seem more intimate.

The shoguns built towering castles with great reception halls. They demanded a bold, impressive new style of painting to express their power. The most talented artists responded by creating large-scale paintings on movable partitions, or screens. The screens were first covered with gleaming *gold leaf* that created a rich halo of light in the dark castle rooms.

The central figure on this screen is Princess Sen, granddaughter of shogun Ieyasu Tokugawas. A musician plays the samisen, a banjolike instrument, to entertain Sen, who has received a letter from her lover, Honda Heihachiro. The painter conveys movement through the lively lines with which he painted the graceful women.

The artist created an unusual interplay between the *foreground* and the *background* to convey a sense of depth. The bold design on the black kimono makes the woman wearing it, who is also lowest in the picture, seem closest to the viewer. The height of the three standing women makes them seem closer than the seated musician, who appears to be smaller and therefore more distant. The long bench on which she sits defines the limits of the room. Golden shapes formed by the outlines of the sumptuous kimonos suggest a luxurious, almost weightless feeling.

The rebirth of Japanese art during the seventeenth century, brought about by the enormous power and wealth of the shoguns, was parallel to the Renaissance revival of art in Europe.

16

BOY PLAYING A FLUTE, about 1630–35
Judith Leyster, Dutch (1609–60), oil on canvas, 29½" x 24¼"

*J*udith Leyster was one of the seventeenth-century Dutch painters who helped establish a taste for pictures celebrating the pleasures of everyday life. These scenes, called genre paintings, appealed to a wide range of people. In her *portrait* of a handsome young flutist, Leyster's artistry transformed what might have been an ordinary picture into a masterpiece.

Leyster built the *composition* with *dynamic* shapes pointing in different directions to create a feeling of motion and energy. Three triangular shapes formed by the skirt of the boy's jacket aim upward, focusing attention on his face and hands. A series of slanted *lines* in the coat, the chair back, the musician's arms, the flute, the violin bow, and the recorder sweep from the lower right to the upper right, focusing attention on a rich variety of tones and textures.

Leyster created a lyrical mood through the expressive way she captured light and shade. She beamed sunlight onto the musician's face and cast his *shadow* onto the wall, thereby creating a feeling of depth. Leyster mirrored the *highlights* and *shading* on his figure with reflected light and with shadows of the instruments in the *background*. Using fine brushstrokes, she created the

Judith Leyster suggests the flutist's musical accomplishment through her expressive portrayal of his hands.

textures of soft velvet and smooth polished wood. With large brushes and bold strokes of golden paint, she created the effect of light gleaming on a rough plaster wall.

Until the twentieth century, two of Leyster's finest works were attributed to a more famous contemporary painter named Frans Hals. She is now recognized as one of the master painters of her time.

19

LOVE IN THE ITALIAN THEATER, 1716
Antoine Watteau, French (1684–1721), oil on canvas, 14½" x 19"

*a*s a young man, Antoine Watteau developed a passion for the musical theater. Before he became a successful painter, applauded for his romantic scenes of fashionable life, Watteau struggled in poverty. His fortune improved when he began to work as a stage designer. Toward the end of his short but glorious career, he painted *Love in the Italian Theater*.

This nocturnal scene suggests a bittersweet moment during the closing performance of a play, when the cast sings the final serenade. Through the balance of light and dark areas, a technique called chiaroscuro, Watteau created a feast of *color* and *texture* that delights the eye.

Watteau illuminated the central figures with blazing torchlight and cast ghostly *shadows* that gradually become inky black, serving to separate the people from the *background*. He painted gleaming *highlights* and *transparent* shadows that convey the silk and velvet fabric in the costumes. Watteau bathed the players on the left in the fiery glow of lantern light and formed rich dark reddish tones that create a sense of drama.

Watteau's skill in *drawing* each of the characters as a distinct personality makes this romantic picture come to life. The realism with which he depicted the old man leaning on his cane, the pretty woman arranging the folds of her robe, and the graceful clown adjusting his cap makes this painting seem like Watteau's tribute to every musician and player who entertained him throughout his life.

Watteau's elegant scene of the musical theater evokes a dreamlike mood of idyllic pleasure.

Antoine Watteau created the effect of torchlight by blending yellow with all of the colors used to depict the guitarist.

THE ORCHESTRA OF THE OPERA, about 1870
Edgar Degas, French (1834–1917), oil on canvas, 22¼" x 18¼"

*E*dgar Degas was captivated by the magnificent scale of the opera: music, drama, song, and ballet performed in a grand theater for a wealthy, sophisticated audience. In this *portrait* of Désiré Dihau, the orchestra's bassoonist, Degas created a picture that was controversial at the time. Rather than painting a formal portrait of a classical artist surrounded by objects that symbolize his talent and intellect, Degas showed Dihau as a working musician.

Degas portrayed Désiré Dihau in realistic detail compared to the blur of color that conveys the dancers onstage.

In *The Orchestra of the Opera,* Degas captured the excitement of being in the front row during a performance. There is so much activity that it is difficult to focus attention on any one person. Some of the participants seem clear and precisely detailed, whereas others are blurred impressions of light, movement, *color,* and *texture.*

Degas brought this scene to life through sharply angled *lines* in the bassoon, the cello, the violin bows, and the neck of the double bass that draw the viewer into the picture. He focuses attention on the orchestra through the *contrast* between the colors and the *detail* with which he painted the musicians, uniformly dressed in black evening clothes, and the vibrant blur of pastel brushstrokes that suggest the twirling ballerinas onstage. Degas abruptly ended, or cropped, the scene below the dancers' heads to create a sense of the distance from the bassoonist to the stage, while the carved top of the bass, called a scroll, visually connects the musicians with the performance.

The Orchestra of the Opera was exhibited once during Degas's lifetime, then disappeared from public view until 1935. Today it is regarded as one of his masterpieces.

THREE MUSICIANS, 1921
Pablo Picasso, Spanish (1881–1973), oil on canvas, 79" x 84¾"

Pablo Picasso is often called the first *modern* painter of the twentieth century because he constantly searched for new and innovative ways to express his creativity. Inspired by his love of African masks and primitive sculpture, Picasso often depicted people as objects made up of geometric shapes: squares, circles, triangles, and rectangles. Contemporary art critics labeled Picasso's almost *abstract* style cubism.

In *Three Musicians*, Picasso constructed a musical trio out of hard-edged shapes using strong *colors* and bold *designs*. He flattened the forms of a rodlike clarinet, a banana-shaped hat, and a cube-shaped room, thereby emphasizing the flatness of the *canvas* on which he painted. Picasso projected jet black *shadows* of the musicians against the *background*, creating a sense of distance from the figures to the rear wall. The solid black shadows, in *contrast* to the array of colors and *textures* in the figures, convey the feeling of afternoon light fading into darkness.

Picasso created a sense of energy and movement by composing the picture using *dynamic forms* that suggest motion through their directional shapes. The violinist's diagonal bow and the diamond pattern of his suit plus the recorder player's slanted hat push the viewers' eyes along a jagged path through the picture. Picasso united the multitude of shapes and patterns with angular zones of cool blue paint that also form the clarinetist's hat and arm and the masklike faces of the fiddler and the singer on the right.

Picasso brought a spirit of fun to this painting that belies the strenuous process of experimentation and discovery that he engaged in every time he faced a blank canvas.

GREEN VIOLINIST, 1923–24
Marc Chagall, Russian (1887–1985), oil on canvas, 78" x 42¾"

The Russian Revolution of 1917 liberated Marc Chagall from religious and artistic oppression. The czars, the former Russian leaders, persecuted Jews and forced them to live in restricted villages called shtetls. After the revolution, Chagall could live where he chose and could express his Jewish heritage through his work. Based on memories of his childhood in the shtetl, he created murals, stage sets, and costumes for the new State Jewish Chamber Theater in Moscow. When Chagall moved to Paris, France, in 1923, he made this version of the *Green Violinist*, originally painted for the theater to symbolize the art of music.

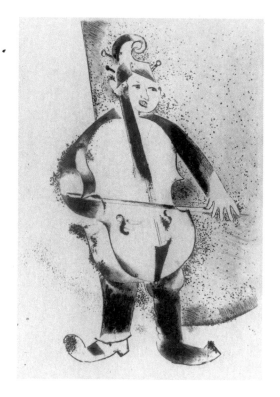

In this etching, Marc Chagall created velvety tones in the cellist's arms and legs with finely etched parallel lines called hatching.

Chagall's fiddler plays high above the village rooftops. Chagall created an otherworldly mood through the thinly painted tones of mauve, gray, blue, and white in the clouds and the buildings. He fashioned the musician's coat in hard-edged purple shapes defined with luminous strokes of lavender. Chagall created a theatrical effect by using bright green paint for the violinist's face and one of his hands.

Chagall painted lively designs based on geometric shapes throughout the *composition*. Squares, such as the little windowpanes in the houses, are echoed in the pattern on the fiddler's trousers. Triangles forming the peaked roofs are mirrored by zigzag folds in the fiddler's purple coat. The curving edges of the coat sweep our eyes from the *foreground* to the sky, where a figure floats happily among circular clouds.

Almost fifty years later, Chagall's joyous vision once again came to life in the theater. The sets and costumes for the 1964 Broadway musical *Fiddler on the Roof* were based directly on this painting.

27

MUSICAL CLOWN, 1938
Walt Kuhn, American (1877–1949), oil on canvas, 40" x 38"

Walt Kuhn sold his first *drawing* to a magazine at age fifteen. He dropped out of school, continued to study painting, and developed a thriving career as a free-lance cartoonist. He also performed as a tap dancer and designed sets and costumes for the theater. While recovering from a severe stomach ulcer in 1925, Kuhn reexamined his life and decided to quit the theater to focus on painting. He began a series of *portraits* of the men and women of the chorus lines, the sideshows, and the orchestras of popular entertainments.

The formal pose, subtle *colors*, and serious expression of this careworn musician creates an aura of dignity. Kuhn conveys a feeling of emotional intensity through the musician's direct gaze and the spare simplicity of the *composition*. He carefully constructed the painting using straight and curved shapes, hard and soft *textures*, light and dark colors. The sweeping vertical shape of the battered tuba is echoed by the tall narrow *form* of the man's face, neck, and chest. Curves shaping the horn's bell are repeated in the top hat. The instrument's complex keys, tubular and metallic, form a *contrast* to the man's graceful fingers, encased in soft suede gloves.

Kuhn used yellow with all of the other hues to create an overall *tone*. He shaped the musician's face with broad strokes of russet painted over a flesh color gleaming with small patches of yellow. *Highlights* on the black jacket are formed with strokes of yellowish gray. In the *background*, patches of purple are neutralized, or made to look gray, with patches of yellow, purple's complementary color.

Kuhn expressed his lifelong romance with show people by incorporating his own features into their portraits. In this picture, Kuhn portrayed the musician's eyes as his own.

MUSIC, 1939
Henri Matisse, French (1869–1954), oil on canvas, 45⅜" x 45⅜"

Henri Matisse was a serious amateur violinist. He often compared the creative process of painting to that of musical composition, using the language of music to describe what he expressed in a painting: harmony, *tone, color*, and balance.

In *Music*, Matisse conveyed the pleasure that music performed in a beautiful room brought him. Matisse gave the *composition* a feeling of order and harmony through the balance and *contrast* of horizontal and vertical *forms*. The elongated figures of the guitarist and singer are the verticals, balanced by three horizontal areas: a band of green leaves, a checkerboard wall in the *background*, and the green base of the sofa in the *foreground*. The slanted edges of the green table invite the viewer into the tranquil scene.

Within this compositional framework, Matisse made the picture sing with colors and *textures*. Although he painted flat areas of color, Matisse created a feeling of depth by balancing warm light hues that appear to come forward, such as the yellow dress and red sofa, with cool dark colors that appear to recede in space, such as the green leaves and black background. He created a variety

of textures, from the sharply etched white *designs* in the cushion and sofa and the border of yellow triangles on the blue dress, to the black background with which he defined the enormous philodendron leaves.

In his journal, Matisse expressed his approach to the art of painting: "Colors have a beauty of their own that must be preserved, as one strives to preserve tonal quality in music. It is a question of organization and construction."

Using charcoal, Henri Matisse created the soft lines, tones, and textures that make this drawing resemble a painting.

STREET MUSICIANS, about 1940
William H. Johnson, American (1901–70), oil on wood, 36⅛" x 28¼"

William H. Johnson was an African-American painter who left South Carolina in 1918 to study at the National Academy of Design in New York City. He developed a vigorous style imitative of the expressive German art of the 1920s, working with big brushes and thick, textured paint. Johnson's personal vision emerged after he spent several years in Tunisia studying the native arts of North Africa during the 1930s.

Returning to New York in 1938, Johnson developed a bold, graphic style and made Harlem a central theme of his work. He felt that by painting in a simplified, posterlike manner, he could more clearly express the joy and sadness of contemporary black life.

Johnson captured a bittersweet moment in his portrayal of two sidewalk entertainers performing for spare change. He painted the figures with sharp black outlines and brilliant shades of yellow, orange, and red that seem even brighter in *contrast* with the areas of solid black. Johnson created a rhythmical interplay between the sharp angular shapes in the woman's stylish hat and jacket and the rounded shapes in her hands and in the guitar. With a few well-observed *lines*, he captured a note of sadness in the faces of the couple who struggle to make ends meet.

Johnson suggested the crisscross black lines of a sidewalk as it might look from an upstairs window. By combining this aerial view with an eye-level view of the couple, Johnson conveys the mood of a constantly changing street scene.

Johnson brought a special insight to being a black American through the themes he chose to depict and through the clarity of his artistic expression.

PORTRAIT OF A MUSICIAN, 1949

Thomas Hart Benton, American (1889–1975), egg tempera on canvas backed with panel, 48¼" x 32⅛"

Thomas Hart Benton drew this portrait with pen and ink, emphasizing the shadows with a few strokes of ink diluted with water, called wash.

Throughout his long career, Thomas Hart Benton was fascinated by musicians as subjects for his paintings. He made on-the-spot *sketches* of musicians while they played, which he later used in his studio as reference material. In this 1949 *portrait*, Benton captured the cool elegance of a Kansas City jazz player engrossed in his music. Through the hazy *background*, Benton suggests the feel of a melancholy blues tune.

By choosing a high vantage point and presenting the bass player in a three-quarter view, Benton exaggerated the rhythmical *contours* with which he composed the figure. He echoed the curved shape of the bass and its f-holes in the performer's necktie and in the elongated folds of his jacket. In contrast, the straight row of strings accentuates the expressive *lines* that convey the man's wiry but strong arms and hands.

Benton used a narrow range of muted colors and painted in egg *tempera*, a material that produces clear light colors that do not darken with age. He built up the hues gradually, using *transparent* dark blue and umber over pale shades of *opaque* ivory and sienna. By adding red to all of the colors except white, Benton created an overall purplish *tone* that recalls the smoky atmosphere of a nightclub. Finally, he painted transparent *shadows* that emphasize the lustrous *highlights* on the figure and the instrument, creating a strong three-dimensional effect.

Benton's last painting of musicians was commissioned by the Country Music Association of Nashville, Tennessee. The day after he completed *The Sources of Country Music* in 1975, Benton died of a heart attack at the age of eighty-five.

DANCE OF THE DOUBLE WOMAN, 1950
Oscar Howe, American Yanktonai Sioux (born 1915), casein on board,
20 ¾" x 19 ¾"

O scar Howe, a Yanktonai Sioux, was born on the Crow-Creek reservation in South Dakota. As a young man, he taught painting to Indian children in exchange for food and a place to live. Howe's dream of making a living as an artist was crushed by poverty and the lack of interest in native arts. After serving in World War II, however, he earned a degree in fine arts through a federal program for war veterans called the GI Bill. Howe later became a professor of art at the University of South Dakota.

Howe embraces a native tradition of the painter as a tribal elder with the responsibility of keeping sacred ceremonies and legends alive. He depicted the Sioux legend of the double woman who materialized as a vision to a drummer during a ritual communication with Wakan Tanka, the supreme spirit. Howe pictured the mystical story through *owa*, a traditional language of painting in which *colors* take their meaning from nature. White, clean and new, expresses the purity of the double woman. Yellow, or sunlight, symbolizes the drummer's spiritual belief. Blue, or sky, represents peace for the Sioux.

Howe used *casein*, a paint known to nomadic cultures for thousands of years, which is made by combining colors made of earth minerals with curdled milk. Because casein is mixed with water and applied with a wet brush, its fluid consistency suits Howe's style of painting with curving outlines, using large areas of flat color, and adding finely detailed decorative emblems.

Howe's clear graphic style expresses a Sioux way of life in which people become one with the sun, the moon, the trees, the hills, and the rocks by living in harmony with nature.

In this watercolor, Fred Kabotie, a Nakayoma Hopi Indian, captured soft textures in the robes and the geometric design of the masks worn by performers dressed as kachinas, or spirit ancestors, of the Hopi tribe.

36

Dance of the Double woman / Oscar Howe

LE-LO-LAI, about 1952–53
Lorenzo Homar, Puerto Rican (born 1913), egg tempera on masonite, 25" x 33"

As a teenager, Lorenzo Homar emigrated with his parents from Puerto Rico to New York City, where he studied painting. On returning to his native land in 1950, Homar was horrified by the poverty there. He voiced his protest in a painting of three gaunt children celebrating *el día de los Reyes*, or Three Kings Day, the happiest day of the Christmas season for most Hispanic children. The children, aged beyond their years by grinding poverty, play and sing a song called "Le-lo-lai."

Lorenzo Homar lit this boy's mask-like face with bright highlights that echo the silver crown.

Homar viewed the musicians from above to display a panoramic view of the shantytown and the glistening sea bathed in iridescent moonlight. He worked in egg *tempera*, a method specially suited to painting precise *details*. Homar blended pure powdered colors, or pigments, with fresh raw egg yolk and enough water to make the paint flow from his brush. He first blocked out the entire scene in flat areas of light colors, which he left uncovered in the little turquoise rooftops.

Using fine brushes and short parallel brushstrokes, Homar then created crisp details and *highlights* and dark *shading* that make the colors resonate. He formed the boys' crowns with silver and *gold leaf*, precious metal foil thinner than tissue paper. He painted *shadows* on top of the gold and the silver to form a three-dimensional effect. Homar created a disquieting mood through the *contrast* between the magnificent crowns and the tragic masklike faces of the children.

Homar has devoted his life to teaching art in Puerto Rico and has inspired thousands of young people to develop their own special talents.

THREE FOLK MUSICIANS, 1967

Romare Bearden, American (1912–88), collage on canvas mounted on board, 50" x 60"

Romare Bearden, an African-American painter who grew up in the South, wove a rich tapestry of childhood memories into his paintings. During visits with his grandmother in Lutherville, Maryland, young Bearden listened to the blues guitar of a local musician named E. C. Johnson. The image of Johnson and the haunting songs he played became etched in Bearden's consciousness. In this painting, Bearden embodies the country blues, a musical form that evolved from the percussive rhythms of West African work songs and from Scotch-Irish folk songs into moving ballads of love and loss.

Bearden created this musical trio by gluing together colored paper and fragments of photographs from magazines, a technique called collage. He carefully arranged eyes, noses, and hands cut out of magazine pictures along with pieces of painted paper to shape the figures. Bearden focused attention on the musicians' eyes and hands by deliberately using images that are too large in proportion to the figures.

Bearden then applied strokes of blue and green paint over the assembled cutouts to create an even blue-gray *tone* in the musicians' faces and clothes. He glued patterned scraps of paper to the *background* to depict a field and a little orange moon rising over the faraway hills. Through the interplay of soft *colors* and *textures* in the figures and flat blocks of intense color in the background, Bearden created a feeling of distance from the *foreground* to the background.

Bearden expressed the joy and surprise of musical improvisation in this collage. Like a gifted blues player who transforms a familiar melody with new energy and emotion, Bearden gives us an exuberant painting created from scraps of discarded paper.

41

IKON HANDS, 1988
Larry Rivers, American (born 1925), oil on canvas on sculpted foam board,
53" x 40¾"

Larry Rivers became a professional saxophone player at age eighteen. Through his friendship with Miles Davis, Rivers became deeply involved in the New York jazz scene. In 1947, he began to study painting seriously and juggled his musical career with his art training. Rivers soon realized that his true talent lay in painting, not in jazz.

With *Ikon Hands*, Rivers chose a close-up view to symbolize the legendary Charlie Parker, widely regarded as one of the greatest jazz musicians of the twentieth century. Rivers captured the ease with which the musician's long elegant fingers span the keys. Through a narrow range of toned-down blues, yellows, and grays, Rivers conjures up the atmosphere of a smoky jazz club.

Rivers combined painting, *drawing* and sculpting to make this relief, an image that projects out from the background. He first made a *charcoal* drawing on *canvas*, which he cut into three pieces: the *background*, which includes the neck of the instrument and its strap; the player's hands; and the bell-shaped horn in the *foreground*. He glued each section onto a lightweight panel called foam board and reassembled the pieces, mounting them onto a wooden frame for stability.

Using pen and ink, the African-American painter Charles White drew a network of fine lines that create an even tone of gray.

He sealed the canvas with a translucent white base coat called gesso that permits the charcoal drawing to show through. Rivers then painted with semi-transparent oil paint, incorporating the *lines* and *shading* of the charcoal drawing into the finished work. In the same way that a brilliant musician makes jazz look easy, Rivers's fluid brushwork gives this painting an effortless feeling.

Rivers, an internationally recognized painter, continues to find time to play the saxophone in the East 13th Street Jazz Band.

FOUR MUSICIANS, 1992

Hung Liu, Chinese (born 1948), mixed media: oil on canvas, lacquered wood, antique architectural pieces, 72" x 96" x 8½"

Hung Liu grew up in China during Mao Tse-tung's Cultural Revolution (1966–76). During that period, the Chinese government used a Confucian proverb, "A woman can hold up half of the sky," to justify using women to perform heavy manual labor. Liu was forced to leave school and work in the fields for four years. In 1984, she emigrated to the United States and began a series of works that depict historical images of China from a woman's perspective.

Although Liu felt oppressed by the Maoist regime, she values her Chinese heritage. Her painting of a religious ritual, based on a nineteenth-century photograph of Buddhist monks, creates a modern shrine for meditation.

Liu constructed this image out of flat and three-dimensional materials. First, she painted the four musicians on *canvas*, using oil paint thinly diluted with *turpentine*. She painted the precisely detailed figures in translucent layers of umber, ocher, and magenta that recall the appearance of an old photograph. Using large brushes, she applied bold strokes of paint on the gong-player's robe and then poured dribbles of paint along the bottom to emphasize that this is a painting, not a photograph.

The antique gold temple carving attached to the canvas above the flutist conveys Liu's respect for religious tradition. She built a shrine into the painting using a plywood box and ordinary objects found in San Francisco's Chinatown. A rice bowl provides the viewer with an empty vessel in which to make a symbolic offering of his or her thoughts.

Liu has said that, for her, the process of creating a painting is a mental excavation. By digging into Chinese history and incorporating traditional images into her paintings, she finds a way to better understand her own past.

An anonymous Japanese painter made the musician disproportionately small to focus attention on Okuni, who originated Japan's Kabuki theater in the sixteenth century.

Glossary and Index

MODERN, 24: A term used to describe ideas, methods, and techniques in art that have been developed in the recent past.

MURAL, 8: A very large painting that decorates a wall or is created as part of a wall. Also called a wall painting.

OPAQUE, 34: Not letting light pass through. Opaque paints conceal what is under them. (The opposite of TRANSPARENT)

PAINT: Artists have used different kinds of paint, depending on the materials that were available to them and the effects they wished to produce in their work.

Different kinds of paint are similar in the way they are made.

1. Paint is made by combining finely powdered pigment with a vehicle. A vehicle is a fluid that evenly disperses the color. The kind of vehicle used sometimes gives the paint its name, for example: oil paint. Pigment is the raw material that gives paint its color. Pigments can be made from natural minerals and from chemical compounds.

2. Paint is made thinner or thicker with a substance called a medium, which can produce a consistency like that of water or mayonnaise or peanut butter.

3. A solvent must be used by the painter to clean the paint from brushes, tools, and the hands. The solvent must be appropriate for the composition of the paint.

ACRYLIC PAINT: Pigment is combined with an acrylic polymer vehicle that is created in a laboratory. By itself, acrylic paint dries rapidly. Several different mediums can be used with acrylic paint: retarders slow the drying process, flow extenders thin the paint, an impasto medium thickens the paint, a gloss medium makes it shiny, a matte medium makes it dull.

Acrylic paint has been popular since the 1960s. Many artists like its versatility and the wide range of colors available. Acrylic paint is also appreciated because its solvent is water, which is non-hazardous.

CASEIN: Pigment is combined with a binder made from milk protein obtained by drying the curd of sour milk. The solvent is water. Because casein paint is brittle when dry, it must be applied to a rigid panel rather than to a flexible canvas to prevent the paint from cracking. A crude form of casein paint made from soured cottage cheese was used in the ancient Egyptian, Greek, Roman, and Hebrew cultures.

OIL PAINT: Pigment is combined with an oil vehicle (usually linseed or poppy oil). The medium chosen by most artists is linseed oil; the solvent is turpentine. Oil paint is never mixed with water. Oils dry slowly, enabling the artist to work on a painting for a long time. Some painters add other materials, such as pumice powder or marble dust, to produce thick layers of color. Oil paint has been used since the fifteenth century. Until the early nineteenth century, artists or their assistants ground the pigment and combined the ingredients of paint in their studios. When the flexible tin tube (like a toothpaste tube) was invented in 1840, paint made by art suppliers became available.

TEMPERA: Pigment is combined with a water-based vehicle. The paint is combined with raw egg yolk to "temper" it into a mayonnaiselike consistency usable with a brush. The solvent for tempera is water. Tempera was used by the ancient Greeks and was the favorite method of painters in medieval Europe. It is now available in tubes, ready to use. The painter supplies the egg yolk.

WATERCOLOR: Pigment is combined with gum arabic, a water-based vehicle. Water is both the medium and the solvent. Watercolor paint now comes ready to use in tubes (moist) or in cakes (dry). Watercolor paint is thinned with water, and areas of paper are often left uncovered to produce highlights.

Gouache is an opaque form of watercolor, which is also called tempera or body color.

Watercolor paint was first used 37,000 years ago by cave dwellers who created the first wall paintings.

PATRON, 12, 14: An individual or organization that supports the arts or an individual artist.

PLASTER, 8: A chalky white powder made of gypsum and lime. When mixed with water it forms a thick paste that dries to a hard finish.

PORTRAIT, 8, 12, 18, 22, 28, 34: A painting, drawing, sculpture, or photograph that represents an individual's appearance and, usually, his or her personality.

SELF-PORTRAIT: 14, A painting of the artist by the artist. *See also* PORTRAIT

SHADING, 8, 14, 18, 38, 42: The use of gradually darker and lighter colors to make an object appear solid and three-dimensional.

SHADOW, 10, 14, 18, 20, 24, 34, 38: An area made darker than its surroundings because direct light does not reach it.

SKETCH, 34: A quickly made drawing.

TEXTURE, 18, 20, 22, 24, 28, 30, 32, 40: The surface quality of a painting. For example, an oil painting could have a thin, smooth surface texture, or a thick, rough surface texture.

TONE, 28, 30, 34, 43, 40: The sensation of an overall coloration in a painting. For example, an artist might begin by painting the entire picture in shades of greenish gray. After more colors are applied using transparent glazes, shadows, and highlights, the mass of greenish gray color underneath will show through and create an even tone, or *tonal harmony*.

Painters working with opaque colors can achieve the same effect by adding one color, such as green, to every other color on their palette. This makes all of the colors seem more alike, or harmonious. The effect of tonal harmony is part of the artist's vision and begins with the first brushstrokes. It cannot be added to a finished painting. *See also* COLOR

TRANSPARENT, 20, 34: Allowing light to pass through so colors underneath can be seen. (The opposite of OPAQUE)

TURPENTINE, 18, 44: A strong-smelling solvent made from pine sap, used in oil painting. *See also* PAINT; OIL PAINT

Credits